# Pog Pops in

Written by Catherine Baker
Illustrated by Nicola Anderson

**Collins**

Tig pins a mat.

Tog pops pads in.

Tig pops pots in.

Tog tips pans in.

Tig sits. Tog sits.

Tig sips. Tog sips.

Tig digs a pit.

Tig digs. Tog naps.

Pog pops in.

Pog naps on Tog.

# Tig taps Pog.

Tog naps. Pog naps.

/g/

14

# After reading

**Letters and Sounds:** Phase 2

**Word count:** 48

**Focus phonemes:** /g/ /o/

**Curriculum links:** Understanding the World; Personal, Social and Emotional development

**Early learning goals:** Reading; use phonic knowledge to decode regular words and read them aloud accurately; demonstrate understanding when talking with others about what they have read

## Developing fluency

- Encourage your child to sound talk and then blend the words as they read e.g. /t/ /i/ /g/ Tig. It may help to point to each sound as your child reads.
- Then ask your child to reread the sentence to support fluency and understanding.
- You could reread the whole book to your child to model fluency and rhythm in the story.

## Phonic practice

- Ask your child to sound talk and blend each of the following words:  t/o/g, t/i/g, p/o/g, p/o/p, p/o/t/s
- Can your child point to the words that have both a /g/ and an /o/ sound in them? (*Tog, Pog*)
- Look at the "I spy sounds" pages (14 and 15). Discuss the picture with your child. Can they find items/ examples of words beginning with the /o/ and /g/ sounds? (*geese, grapes, golf, gate, goal, octopus, ostrich, orange, ocean, over*)

## Extending vocabulary

- Ask your child:
  o What does the word **sips** mean on page 7? (*drinks*)
  o Can you think of any other words that mean "to drink"? (*slurp, gulp, glug*)
  o Discuss the difference between "sip" and "gulp" with your child. (*Sip is drinking small amounts at a time slowly, gulp is drinking large amounts at a time quickly*)